W9-DJI-846

FREE LIBRARY OF
SPRINGFIELD TOWNSHIP

FREE LIBRARY OF
SPRINGFIELD TOWNSHIP

The CHERRY TREE

written by **DAISAKU IKEDA** · illustrated by **BRIAN WILDSMITH**

English version by Geraldine McCaughrean

Alfred A. Knopf   New York

TAICHI AND HIS SISTER, Yumiko, lived with their mother in an abandoned farmhouse. Their country had been at war, and airplanes had dropped bombs on their village. Their own house lay in ruins, and their father was dead. For Taichi and Yumiko, the bombs had shattered their world into a thousand pieces. Their mother's heart was shattered too.

Every morning Mother walked the long road into town to earn a little money shining shoes. The children waved good-bye to her. How empty the house felt after she was gone! It was better to be outside playing.

When Taichi and Yumiko were with other children, they could pretend everything was all right, that Mother was at home cooking dinner. They could make believe they were building her a fine new house. If they pretended hard enough, the heap of rubble that they played on could be a mountain, an island, a ship, or a castle.

"Here comes a fierce tiger to guard my door!" cried Yumiko. But it was only a small stray cat. Yumiko and Taichi made a special friend of that lonely little cat. When he wandered away one day, they searched for hours until they found him in a place where they had never been before.

The little cat was sitting in the bare branches of a sickly tree. An old man was busily wrapping the tree's trunk in straw matting.

"What are you doing?" asked Yumiko.

"Winter's coming," said the old man. "I must take care of her. Trees feel the cold too, you know. If it snows, she could die!"

"The tree looks dead already," said Taichi.

"Not quite. It's true she hasn't blossomed since before the war. But one day, with a little kindness and patience, she may again. Not in my lifetime, perhaps, but one day! I'm sure of it. But I must hurry...if only I weren't so old and slow." And he went back to bandaging the wounded tree.

Yumiko could not forget the old man and the ugly, knobbled tree. That night she lay awake thinking about them. In the darkness, she heard Taichi whisper, "Mother, we met the oddest man today. He takes care of an old, sick cherry tree, hoping that one day it will blossom again. Do you suppose it ever could?"

"It never hurts to hope," Mother replied. "Perhaps you could help the old man."
"Yes, let's help!" cried Yumiko. She turned over and went to sleep, while
moonlight tumbled in through the window.

The same moon shone down on the old cherry tree that night. Among the damaged roots, beneath the bare branches, friends gathered. For many years, foxes, badgers, owls, and other animals had been sheltered by the tree.

The next day, after Mother had gone off to work, Taichi and Yumiko left their home. Not a word was spoken, but they both knew where they were going. There was snow in the clouds and ice on the wind. They must hurry if they were to help the old man save the tree.

All day long they dressed the sorry-looking branches in scarves of straw.

The little cat kept them company. "I believe you brought us here to meet the cherry tree!" said Yumiko. The only reply was a purr.

When the first snow fell, Yumiko and Taichi climbed up the hill and tenderly
brushed the snow away from the tree's branches. Then they called on the old man
and told him what they had done. He put on his hat and went out in the snow
with them.

"I did hope someone would remember the tree!" he exclaimed. "I was so worried when the snow came early and fell so hard. But I never gave up hope, and you see I was right! Along came two kind children to help me. One day the cherry tree will blossom again. You mark my words!"

"I hope so," said Taichi, but he did not feel very sure.

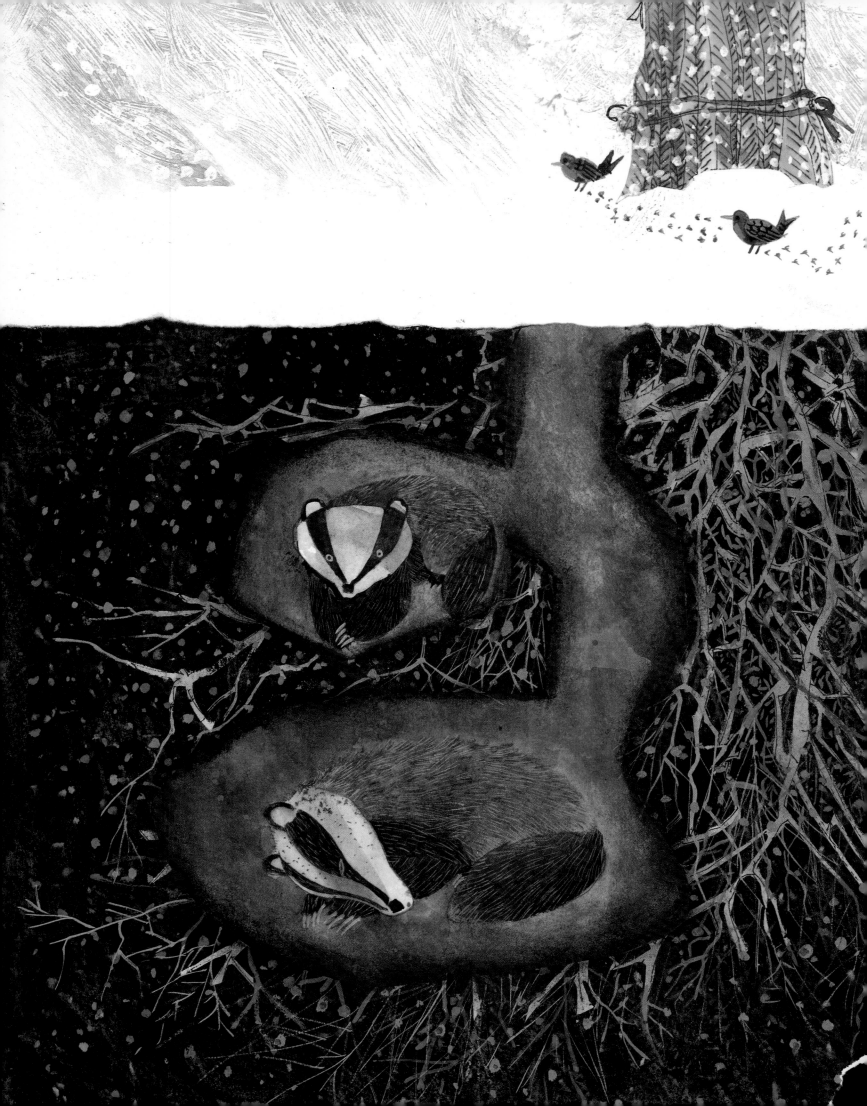

Soon the winter was too fierce and cruel for anyone to visit the cherry tree: not the old man, nor the cat, nor the children. Even the wild animals hid in their dens, deep beneath knotty roots frozen in the icy ground. Everyone was watching for spring and an end to the killing cold.

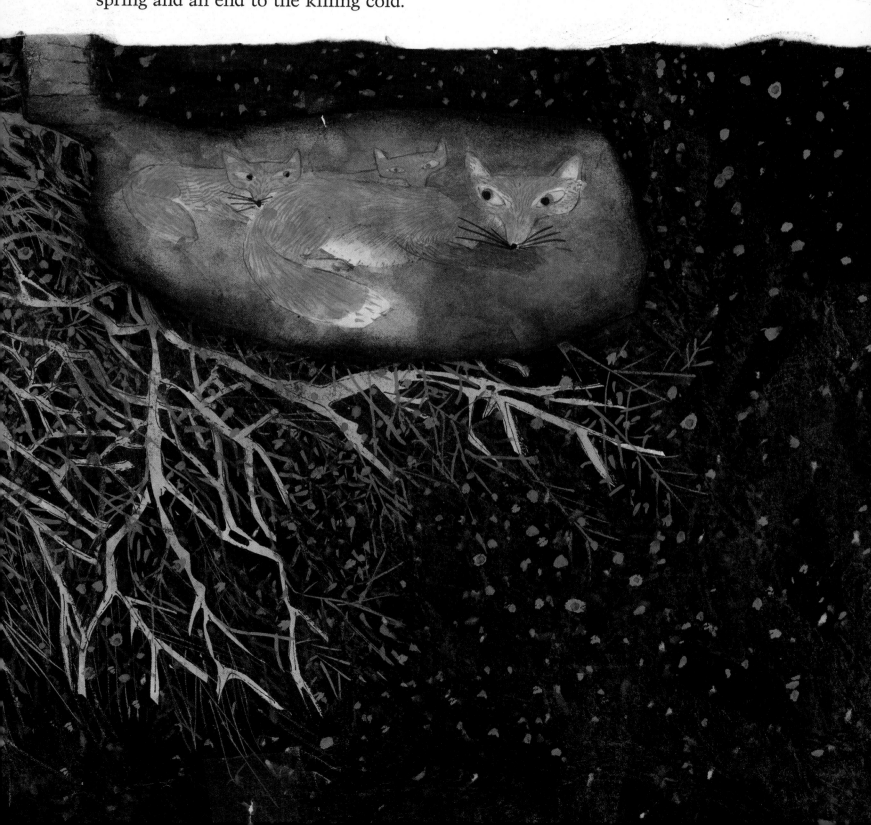

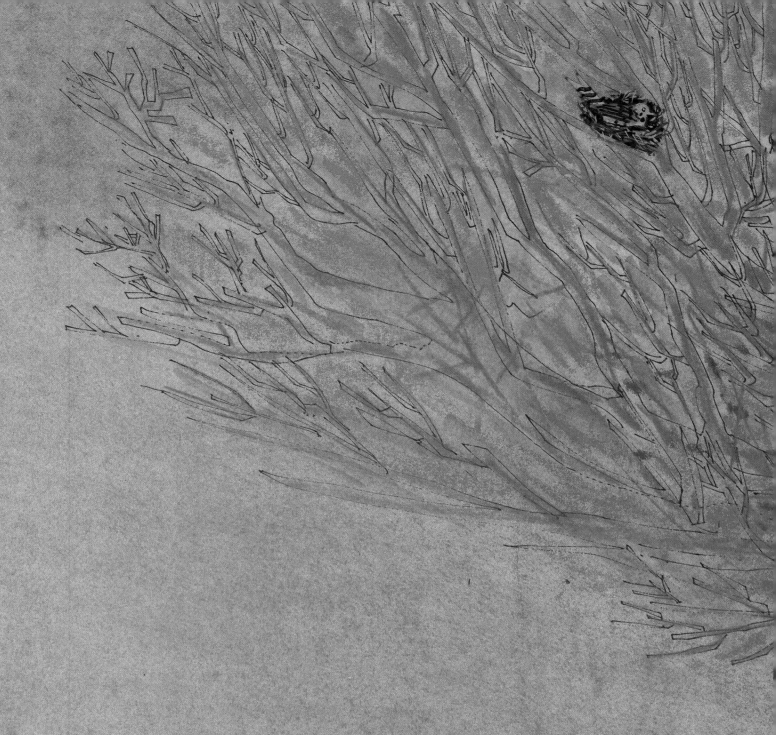

Spring came at last.

Yumiko and Taichi peeled off the wrappers of straw, and the cherry tree stood as bare and brown as before.

"Oh, I hope it blossoms this year!" said Taichi.

"I've said that now for many, many years," said the old man.

"But we can hope, can't we?" said Yumiko.

"Of course! That's the marvelous thing about hope."

Was it Yumiko who saw it first, or was it Taichi? Perhaps it was the old man, or even the cat. But one spring morning, as they stood staring up into the tree, the first pink blossom opened its petals to the sun.

Suddenly the tree was a cloud of petals—a froth of flowers. The cherry tree had come back to life!

Yumiko and Taichi brought their mother to see the blossoms. She said that it did her good to see such loveliness. That very day her broken heart began to mend.

People came from all over to see the tree.

"I remember it now!" said someone. "It used to blossom like this before the war, but I'd given up hope that it would ever bloom again."

"Oh, you should never give up hope," said Yumiko.

"Never!" echoed Taichi.

In time, the village also came back to life. New houses and shops were built. Mother found work in a shop, so she no longer needed to walk the weary road into town each day, or leave the children on their own. Life was everything they had dared to hope for. As their friend the old man said, "With love and patience, nothing is impossible. I should hope you know that by now."

THIS IS A BORZOI BOOK PUBLISHED BY ALFRED A. KNOPF, INC.

Text copyright © 1991 by Daisaku Ikeda
English version copyright © 1991 by Geraldine McCaughrean
Illustrations copyright © 1991 by Brian Wildsmith
All rights reserved under International and Pan-American Copyright Conventions. Published in
the United States by Alfred A. Knopf, Inc., New York. Distributed by Random House, Inc.,
New York. Originally published in Great Britain by Oxford University Press in 1991.
First American edition 1992

Manufactured in Hong Kong   10 9 8 7 6 5 4 3 2 1

Library of Congress Cataloging-in-Publication Data
McCaughrean, Geraldine. The cherry tree / by Daisaku Ikeda ; English version by Geraldine
McCaughrean ; illustrated by Brian Wildsmith.   p. cm.
Summary: After a war destroys their Japanese village and kills their father, Taichi and Yumiko
find hope by nursing a cherry tree through a harsh winter and seeing it blossom into new life.
ISBN 0-679-82669-6 (trade)   ISBN 0-679-92669-0 (lib. bdg.)
[1. Trees—Fiction. 2. War—Fiction. 3. Japan—Fiction.]   I. Ikeda, Daisaku. Sh⁻onen to sakura.
II. Wildsmith, Brian, ill.   III. Title.   PZ7.M4784133Ch   1992   [E]—dc20   91-22148

E
McCAUGHREAN
THE CHERRY TREE   15.00

93

S   X

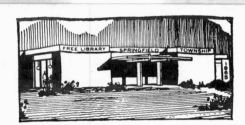

**FREE LIBRARY OF
SPRINGFIELD TOWNSHIP**
1600 Paper Mill Road
Wyndmoor, Penna. 19118
836-5300

DEMCO

The cherry tree /
E McCa   3530000
                                          25058
I

FREE LIBRARY OF
SPRINGFIELD TOWNSHIP